Tom and Ricky

and the

Thief in the Brown Van

Bob Wright

High Noon Books
Nov

The Thief in the Brown Van

Bob Wright
AR B.L.: 2.1
Points: 0.5   UG

Cover Design: Nancy Peach
Interior Illustrations: Herb Heidinger

Glossary: missing, baseball, dirty, idea, chase, always, bump, number, town, people, coach

International Standard Book Number: 0-87879-339-9

7   6   5   4
19 18 17 16 15 14 13

High Noon Books

a division of ATP
20 Commercial Blvd.
Novato, California 94949

Contents

CHAPTER 1

Missing Dogs

It was Saturday. Tom and Ricky sat in the front room. They were at Ricky's house. They didn't say anything. They just looked at the rain. It didn't stop. It just kept on raining. Patches, Ricky's dog, was sleeping.

"Where's the sun? Why doesn't it stop raining?" Ricky asked.

"I don't know. It was nice all week. Now look at it. Rain, rain, rain," Tom said.

"I was going to the park today," Ricky said.

"I was, too. Now they won't have try-outs for baseball. It's too wet," Ricky said.

The phone rang. Ricky went to answer it. It was Ann. Ricky talked to her. Then he went back into the front room. Tom was still looking at the rain.

"Who was it?" Tom asked.

"It was Ann. Buck is missing," Ricky said.

Buck was Ann's dog. He was a little dog. He liked to stay home.

"Buck is not like that. He would not run away," Tom said.

"I know. Buck is a good dog. He likes to stay near Ann," Ricky said.

"Look! The rain is stopping," Tom said.

Ricky jumped up.

Patches woke up. He wagged his tail.

"Let's go over to see Ann. Maybe we can help her find Buck," Ricky said.

"We might see him. He might be near Ann's house," Tom said.

"Mom, we're going to ride over to Ann's house," Ricky called out.

Ricky's mother came into the front room. "I don't want you to go out in that rain," she said.

"It stopped. We won't get wet," Ricky said.

"OK. But don't be gone too long. The rain might start again," she said.

Patches jumped up. He wanted to go, too.

"OK, Patches. Come on," Ricky said.

They got on their bikes. Patches ran in back of them down the street.

"Look! There's Eddie," Tom called out.

"What's he doing? He's all wet," Ricky said.

Eddie was standing next to his bike. He was looking up and down the street. He didn't see Tom and Ricky.

"Eddie! Eddie!" Ricky called out.

Eddie saw them. Tom and Ricky rode over to him.

"What are you doing? You're all wet," Ricky said.

"Are you looking for Buck?" Tom asked.

"Buck? No, I'm looking for Lucky, my dog," Eddie said.

"What do you mean?" Tom asked.

"Is Lucky missing, too?" Ricky asked.

"Tell me about Buck," Eddie said.

"Is Lucky missing, too?"

"Ann can't find him. She has looked and looked for him," Ricky said.

"Lucky is missing. Buck is missing. Is it the rain?" Eddie asked.

"It can't be. Patches is still here," Tom said.

Patches wagged his tail. He seemed to know what they were saying.

"Come on. Let's get over to Ann's house," Tom said.

"Where does she live?" Eddie asked.

"Right over there," Tom answered.

They all walked over to Ann's house. Patches was right with them.

"Stop. I think I hear Dave," Eddie said.

CHAPTER 2

A Dirty Baseball Cap

Dave was yelling. But he wasn't calling the boys. He was calling his dog.

"Trapper! Trapper! Here Trap! Come here," he called out.

Dave started to go away. He didn't see Tom, Ricky, Eddie, and Patches.

"Dave. Stop. We want to talk to you," Ricky called to him.

Dave stopped. He saw all of them.

"Where's Trapper?" Ricky asked.

"I wish I knew. He ran out to play. I haven't seen him all day," Dave answered.

"Where have you looked?" Eddie asked.

"Everywhere. I've been looking everywhere for him. I just can't find him," Dave answered.

"Maybe he just ran away," Tom said.

Ann could hear all of them talking. She came out of her house. "What's going on?" she asked.

"Come on. Let's go see Ann," Ricky said.

They all walked over to Ann's house.

"What are all of you doing out here?" Ann asked.

"Tom and I wanted to help you find Buck. Then we saw Eddie and Dave," Ricky said.

"Lucky is missing," Eddie said.

"And so is Trapper," Dave said.

"We're looking for our dogs. But we can't find them," Eddie said.

"Have you looked for Buck?" Eddie asked Ann.

"Yes. I let him out of the house. He didn't come back. He always comes back," Ann said.

"That's what I did. I let Lucky out. He always comes back. This time he didn't," Eddie said.

"What about you, Dave?" Ann asked.

"I was in the park with Trapper. He was looking at all the birds. He ran over into some trees. But he didn't come back," Dave said.

"Did you look for him?" Tom asked.

"You bet I did. I looked and looked. But I didn't find him," Dave answered.

"Where did you look, Ann?" Tom asked.

"I went over to Mrs. Gold's house. She lives down the street. Buck likes to go there. She gives him bones," Ann said.

"Was Buck there?" Ricky asked.

"No, he wasn't," she answered.

"Did you see anyone when you went home?" Eddie asked.

"I saw a truck parked down the street. A tall man was getting into it. I ran over to him. I asked if he had seen a little black dog. He said he didn't see anything," she said.

"How about you, Eddie? Did you see anything?" Ricky asked.

"Yes, I did. Come to think of it, I did. I saw a man getting into a van. It was brown. But he went away fast. I didn't ask him anything," Eddie answered.

"Stop! I didn't see a truck. I saw a van. It was a brown van," Ann said.

"Maybe it was the same one that Eddie saw," Dave said.

"There are a lot of brown vans in this town," Eddie said.

"Did you see anyone in it?" Tom asked.

"Yes. I saw a man. He was tall and thin. He had on a dirty baseball cap," Ann said.

Eddie jumped up. "The man I saw in the brown van looked like that. He was tall and thin. He had on a dirty baseball cap."

"He was tall and thin. He had on a dirty baseball cap."

CHAPTER 3

A Good Idea

Patches jumped up when Eddie jumped up. Patches started barking.

"Stop it, Patches," Ricky said.

"What's going on? Ann and Eddie can't find their dogs. They saw a man in a brown van. The man they saw had on a dirty baseball cap," Ricky said.

Dave didn't say anything. He knew that Trapper was gone. But he didn't see the brown van. Or the man.

"That does it. We have to do something."
Tom said.

"What?" Dave asked.

"I say we go to the police and tell them,"
Ricky said.

"Dave and I will ride around. We'll try to
find that brown van," Eddie said.

"I'll go with you," Ann said.

"Tom and I will go to the police," Ricky
said.

"That's a good idea. Sergeant Collins will
help us," Tom said.

They all got on their bikes. Patches started
to bark. "OK, Patches. You come with us,"
Ricky said.

Ann, Eddie, and Dave started to look everywhere for the brown van. Tom and Ricky went as fast as they could to the police.

"You know what, Ricky?" Tom called out.

"No, what?" Ricky answered.

"I don't see any dogs," Tom said.

CHAPTER 4

Sergeant Collins Helps Out

Tom and Ricky rode as fast as they could go. Patches ran fast, too. They knew Sergeant Collins would help them if he was there.

They jumped off their bikes. "I don't have my lock," Tom said.

"That's OK. There are a lot of police here. It will be OK," Ricky said.

"What about Patches?" Tom asked.

"He'll be OK. Patches, sit. We'll be back," Ricky said. Patches sat down by the bikes.

They ran in as fast as they could. They didn't see Sergeant Collins. There were a lot of police there.

"Can you tell us where Sergeant Collins is?" Ricky said to one man.

"Just go down this hall. You'll see him," the man said.

"There he is," Tom yelled. They ran over to Sergeant Collins.

"I haven't seen you two in a long time," Sergeant Collins said.

"Sergeant Collins, we have to tell you about all the dogs," Tom said. Tom and Ricky talked at the same time. Sergeant Collins looked at them. He was all mixed up.

"Stop. Tell it all to me again. I am all mixed up," Sergeant Collins said.

Ricky told everything. He didn't go fast. "Did I say everything, Tom?" he asked.

"That's it," Tom said.

Sergeant Collins didn't say anything. He just looked at Tom and Ricky. Then he said, "This is a mystery. Something is not right."

"What do you think?" Ricky asked.

"We had something like this ten years ago," he said.

"Do you think you can help us?" Tom asked.

"I hope I can," Sergeant Collins said.

"What do you want us to do?" Ricky asked.

"Can we help?" Tom asked.

"Did you or anyone get the number on the van?" the Sergeant asked.

"No. Everything was too fast," Ricky said.

"We had something like this ten years ago," he said.

"Let's do this. Go back to the park. Look around. You might see that brown van. Get the number if you do. Then come back here," the Sergeant said.

"Is that all you want us to do?" Tom said.

"That will help me a lot," the Sergeant said.

"We'll be back as soon as we can," Ricky said.

They ran to the front door. They stopped and looked out. It was still wet. But, it wasn't raining. There were not many cars. They saw a van parked down the street. Then it started to go.

"Look at that van. Eddie was right. There must be a lot of them in this town," Tom said.

"And it's a brown one, too," Ricky said.

They got on their bikes. Then Ricky said, "Where's Patches? He was sitting right here when we went in."

"Patches! Patches!" Tom called out.

Patches did not come. They called and called.

"Tom, I don't like this. Where's Patches? Now he's missing," Ricky said.

CHAPTER 5

The Chase

"Come on, Patches. Come on," Tom called.

"It's no use, Tom. Now he's missing," Ricky said.

"That van, Ricky. I bet it was that same brown van," Tom said.

"It all adds up. That brown van is always near when a dog is missing," Ricky said.

"What do we do?" Tom asked.

"You go after that van. See where it is going. I'll get Sergeant Collins," Ricky said.

Tom got on his bike. He went as fast as he could.

Ricky ran back and got Sergeant Collins.

"Sergeant Collins! Sergeant Collins! Patches is missing. We saw the brown van. Tom is going after it," Ricky said.

"Now we can do something," the Sergeant said. He jumped up.

"What are you going to do?" Ricky asked.

"Come with me. I need you," he said.

Sergeant Collins ran to his car. Ricky was right with him. "Get in. What way did the van go?" he asked Ricky.

"That way," Ricky said.

"Why aren't you going fast?" Ricky asked.

"He will see me, if I go fast. Then he will go fast, too," the Sergeant said.

"I don't see the van," Ricky said.

"We'll just have to find it. It has to be near here," the Sergeant said.

"Stop. There's Tom. He sees us. He wants to tell us something," Ricky said.

Tom was standing by his bike. Sergeant Collins pulled his car up next to Tom. He called out to Tom.

"Where is the van?"

"Down that way. He isn't going fast. I could go as fast as he was going," Tom said.

"I'm going to stay with Sergeant Collins and help him," Ricky said.

"What should I do?" Tom asked.

"Go back and tell Ann, Eddie, and Dave, what we're doing. We're going to get their dogs. Let them know everything will be OK," the Sergeant said.

"OK. Good luck," Tom called out.

Sergeant Collins didn't talk much now. He was looking for the van. He wanted to get it. He wanted to find out about the dogs.

"There it is. I can see it," Ricky said.

"I see it, too," the Sergeant said.

"Why don't you go faster?" Ricky asked.

"I don't want him to know we're after him. He is staying on Front Street. Front Street goes to the next town," the Sergeant said.

The police car was getting near the van. Front Street was an old street. It had a lot of bumps. The van was not going fast. But it was going up and down. So was the police car. The man in the van didn't seem to know that the police car was in back of him. Just then the brown van went over a big bump in the street. The back doors opened.

"Look at that," Ricky said.

The van was full of dogs. And the dog right by the door was Patches. All the dogs were barking.

"That's Patches. That's him. Go faster, Sergeant Collins. We have to get Patches," Ricky yelled.

"I can't go too fast. Patches might fall out. I might hit him. There are too many dogs in that van," the Sergeant said.

Patches wagged his tail. Then he jumped.

There were too many bumps. The van could not go fast. Ricky called out, "Patches! Patches! Jump, boy."

Patches saw Ricky. He didn't want to jump. But he wanted to be with Ricky. He barked. He wagged his tail. Then he jumped.

CHAPTER 6

Going After the Thief

Sergeant Collins stopped his car. Ricky jumped out. He ran over to Patches. He made sure that Patches was all right. Patches was OK. He could have been hurt. Patches licked Ricky's face.

"What about the van? Where is it?" Ricky asked.

"He got away. But I got his number. I'll call it in from the car," Sergeant Collins said.

Sergeant Collins took Ricky and Patches back to Ann's house. Everyone was there.

"It sure is good to see you, Patches," Tom said.

Ricky told them how they got Patches.

"What about the van and our dogs?" Eddie asked.

"We'll get that van. I got the number," Sergeant Collins said,

"Did you see Buck in the back of the van?" Ann asked.

"I didn't see Buck or Lucky or Trapper," Ricky said.

"There were a lot of dogs in that van," the Sergeant said.

"They could have been there. We just didn't see them," Ricky said.

The Sergeant looked at all the kids. They all wanted their dogs back. "I think your dogs are all right. I think I know what's going on."

"You do? Tell us what you think," Eddie said.

"That van was on Front Street. Front Street goes to the next town. They have a lot of dogs in that town. A lot of them don't have homes. They have a man who gets those dogs," the Sergeant said.

"How does he know if the dogs don't have a home?" Dave asked.

"He looks to see if they have a tag on them," the Sergeant said.

"What if they don't have a tag?" Ann asked.

"Then he gets $5.00 for each dog," the Sergeant said.

"But our dogs have tags," Ann said.

"I know they do. But this man cuts them off," the Sergeant said.

"He comes to our town. He gets our dogs. He takes all the dogs he can find," Dave said.

"Then he cuts off their tags," Ricky said.

"And then he gets $5.00 for each dog," Ann said.

"And then he gets rich," Tom said.

"And then we don't have our dogs anymore," Ricky said.

"Yes, it is very bad," Sergeant Collins said.

"Where are all the dogs now?" Ricky asked.

"I don't know. The man might keep them for two or three days," the Sergeant said.

"Can we help find them?" Tom asked.

"I will go there. You all stay here. It won't look good if we all go," the Sergeant said.

"How will you find them?" Ann asked.

"I'll ask around. I know some people there. They might know something. The people of that town are nice. They won't like this," the Sergeant said.

"I still want to help find Lucky," Eddie said.

"I know you do. And Ann and Dave want to get their dogs. I don't want that man to see all of you with me. He might do something bad. He might hurt your dogs," the Sergeant said.

"That's right. We don't want the dogs to get hurt," Eddie said.

"Let's do this. I'll take Tom and Ricky. They can help me. Is that all right with the rest of you?" the Sergeant asked.

"It's OK with me," Ann said.

"With me, too," Eddie said.

Dave said it was all right with him.

"Well, then, let's go," Sergeant Collins said.

Tom and Ricky got in the police car. Ricky called back to Eddie, "Take care of Patches for me."

CHAPTER 7

Ready for the Thin Man

The police car took off. This time it was going fast. They had to go fast. They had to get the dogs before they were hurt.

The car went on to Front Street. This was the way to the next town. That's where the dogs were.

"I hope Lucky, Buck, and Trapper are all right," Sergeant Collins said.

"Do you think they might be hurt?" Ricky asked.

"I don't know. They could be," he answered.

They were going down Front Street very fast.

"This is not a good street. They have to fix it," Tom said.

"It has too many bumps," Ricky said.

"The bumps are good," the Sergeant said.

"Good?" Tom asked.

"They made the doors of the van open. That's how we got Patches back," he said.

"That's right, Tom. It's good to have Patches back. I'll take the bumps any day," Ricky said.

Sergeant Collins stopped the car. They were at the next town.

The Sergeant didn't say anything.

"What do we do now?" Ricky asked.

"We need to get some answers," the Sergeant said.

"How do we do that?" Ricky asked.

"There's a man. I'm going to talk to him. You stay here," he said. Sergeant Collins got out of the car. He went over to the man. They talked. Then he came back.

"Did you find out anything?" Tom asked.

"I sure did. That man has lived in this town for a long time. He knows a man who lives in a big house near here. That man has a lot of dogs. And the man has a brown van!" the Sergeant said.

"A brown van! That's him. That's the thin man with the dirty baseball cap," Ricky said.

"How do we get there?" Tom asked.

"I know the way. It's near here," he said.

The police car didn't go fast this time. Sergeant Collins didn't want the thin man to know they were coming.

"That's it. Look," he said. Then he stopped the car.

Tom and Ricky saw a big, old white house. There was a little house near it. The big house was away from other houses. There were a lot of trees around it. They could hear a lot of dogs barking.

"I can hear the dogs," Ricky said.

"That's why he lives here. He has to be alone. He has too many dogs. They bark a lot," the Sergeant said.

"Look. There's the brown van," Tom said.

"He must be in the house," the Sergeant said.

"What do we do now?" Ricky asked.

"Let's see if he is alone. Maybe we can get him," the Sergeant said.

They didn't go fast. They stayed low. They got to the side of the big house.

"You look in, Ricky," the policeman said.

"He's there," Ricky said.

"Good. Now we can get him," the Sergeant said.

CHAPTER 8

Lucky Dogs

Sergeant Collins went to the front door of the big house. The door didn't open. He gave it a big kick. Down it went.

The thin man jumped up. His dirty cap fell to the floor. He didn't know what to do. Sergeant Collins walked over to him. The thin man picked up a baseball bat.

"Stay where you are," the thin man said.

"Put that bat down," the Sergeant said.

"What do you want?" the thin man said.

"I want you and I want the dogs," the Sergeant said.

"You can't take my dogs," the man said.

"Put that bat down. I have two more men."

"Put that bat down. I have two more men. You'll never get away from here," the Sergeant said.

"Two more men? OK. OK. I give up. What's the use? You can take the dogs," he said. He put the bat down.

"Come with me." Sergeant Collins took him to the car and locked him in. Then he came back.

"We've got him. Now let's see how the dogs are," he said to Tom and Ricky.

They walked over to the little house. They all looked in. It was full of dogs. They were all dirty. They needed food and water.

"I see Buck and Trapper," Ricky said.

"And there's Lucky," Tom said.

"I think we can take them back with us. I'll call the police in this town to get the rest," the Sergeant said.

All the dogs wagged their tails when Tom and Ricky got the three dogs out. "I wish we could take all of them," Ricky said.

"They'll all be out of here today," the Sergeant said. "They'll be all right."

When they got back to the car, Ricky said, "Where will we put the dogs?"

"They can go in back with the thin man," the Sergeant said. The dogs jumped in the back seat. They barked at the man all the way back home.

Eddie and Dave were at Ann's house. They all ran to the police car when they saw the dogs.

The sun was out now. Everyone was happy. The dogs jumped all over the kids.

"I have to take this man with me. Thank you for helping me. The dogs will all be OK," Sergeant Collins said.

"You know what?" Ricky said.

"What?" the Sergeant asked.

"That man made Tom and me miss the baseball try-outs. Now we can't get on the team."

'Sure you can," the Sergeant answered.

They all looked at Sergeant Collins.

"Are you sure?" Ricky asked.

"Sure I'm sure. I'm the coach. And I missed them, too!"